MARVEL

CIVIL WAR
CAPTAIN AMERICA

THE JUN

© 2016 MARVEL

Excerpt from *Phase Two: Marvel's Captain America: The Winter Soldier* copyright © 2016 MARVEL

Little, Brown and Company

Hachette Book Group
1290 Avenue of the Americas, New York, NY 10104
Visit us at lb-kids.com

Little, Brown and Company is a division of Hachette Book Group, Inc.
The Little, Brown name and logo are trademarks of Hachette Book Group, Inc.

The publisher is not responsible for websites (or their content) that are not owned by the publisher.

First Edition: April 2016

Library of Congress Control Number: 2016932122

ISBN 978-0-316-27142-4

10 9 8 7 6 5 4 3 2 1

RRD-C

Printed in the United States of America

MARVEL
CIVIL WAR
CAPTAIN AMERICA

THE JUNIOR NOVEL

ADAPTED BY CHRIS WYATT

BASED ON THE SCREENPLAY BY
CHRISTOPHER MARKUS & STEPHEN McFEELY

PRODUCED BY KEVIN FEIGE

DIRECTED BY ANTHONY AND JOE RUSSO

LITTLE, BROWN AND COMPANY
New York   Boston

PRELUDE

One day, creatures from beyond space came through a portal in the sky and attacked New York City.

The alien monsters, called Chitauri, were strong and armed with powerful weapons that were years ahead of human technology. They were assisted by Loki, a godlike being who had prepared the way for their attack.

With an enemy army that overwhelming, New York should have been crushed.

But that was not what happened.

Instead, when that day came—a day unlike any other—Earth's mightiest heroes found themselves united against a common threat.

That day, the Avengers were born.

They defeated the Chitauri, saving New York and, without a doubt, all mankind. The world recognized the Avengers as heroes.

The Avengers were easy to admire:

Captain America—a legendary Super-Soldier from another time;

Iron Man—a genius billionaire inventor who had created his own robotic armor;

Thor—a valiant warrior from the golden realm of Asgard;

Black Widow—a spy with expert-level training;

Hawkeye—a trusted government agent and the world's best archer;

And the Hulk—a Goliath-like raging monster.

But the world's love affair with the Avengers was not without complications.

Not long after what became known as the Battle of New York, Captain America discovered that S.H.I.E.L.D., the US intelligence organization that brought the Avengers together, had actually been used as a front for a terrorist group called Hydra. Hydra had infiltrated S.H.I.E.L.D. in the organization's very beginnings.

Captain America was able to expose Hydra and send its agents running, but only after bringing down three massive floating warships called Helicarriers—which crashed into Washington, DC. The devastation was enormous.

Later, the Hulk—who had saved so many in

New York—went on an unexplained rampage in the South African city of Johannesburg. Hulk destroyed several city blocks before his own teammate, Iron Man, used special Hulkbuster armor to contain him.

On top of that, Tony Stark—the man inside the Iron Man suit—and Bruce Banner—the human identity of the Hulk—created a rogue robot called Ultron. Tony had intended for Ultron to become Earth's ultimate defense against more attacks by the Chitauri or other powerful aliens. However, due to an evil outside influence, Ultron became a killing machine—and attacked the entire planet. Tony's creation was determined to drive human beings into extinction.

The Avengers chased Ultron and his newly created robot army across the globe. Their final showdown devastated a small Baltic country named Sokovia.

Because of the events in Sokovia and everything that went before it, the world was no longer willing to accept the Avengers as model heroes and wanted a plan of action to avoid future destruction.

It didn't help public perception when the Avengers' lineup drastically changed. Thor returned to his home of Asgard. Bruce Banner suddenly disappeared, never facing any real consequences for what the Hulk did in Johannesburg. Hawkeye—Clint Barton—went into retirement and focused on spending time with his family. Even Iron Man seemed less involved with the team.

So, Captain America and Black Widow started training a team of new recruits, made up of heroes the public had a harder time trusting:

Scarlet Witch—a Sokovian refugee who possessed strange magic-like abilities;

Vision—a synthetic humanoid created by Ultron using the remains of another android;

War Machine—an ex–US Marine in a heavily armored iron suit, sometimes referred to as a one-man army;

And Falcon—an ex-soldier who flew through the air using a jet-powered wing suit.

Together, this team was a powerful force, but they found themselves under the same scrutiny and suspicion as the original Avengers. The leaders of the world were left with many questions about the new Avengers. Why couldn't more lives have been saved in Washington, DC; Johannesburg; and Sokovia? How could they prevent another cataclysm? And what help could they offer the Avengers in keeping the world safe while also mitigating collateral damage?

Having a team of Super Heroes ready to defend the planet had obvious advantage, but only if those Super Heroes did more good than harm.

CHAPTER 1

Wanda Maximoff sat in a café in Lagos, Nigeria, sipping her tea and trying to look normal.

She was anything but normal.

As a child in Sokovia, she and her brother lost their parents, and almost died, too, because of a bomb manufactured by Stark Industries. Growing up, Wanda was completely devoted to the idea of getting revenge on American weapon builders in general—and Tony Stark in particular. She was so committed to her vendetta that she let a maniacal scientist from Hydra experiment on her body: The scientist wanted to give her super-powers, to make her into a living weapon of mass destruction.

It worked.

Wanda, a.k.a. Scarlet Witch, became one of the Enhanced. She gained powers that enabled her to move and manipulate objects with the sheer force of her mind, read people's thoughts and memo-ries, and inflict crippling psychological manipu-lations. She could also levitate and shoot energy blasts from her hands, which allowed her to strike precise hits against her enemies. She had intended to use all those abilities to destroy Tony Stark and the Avengers, but she had a change of heart.

During the battle with Ultron, she had seen

Iron Man and the other American heroes in a new light. Soon she found herself battling beside them to save as many lives as she could from Ultron's killer robot army.

And now she was an Avenger, too! She had become a member of the very organization she had once hoped to destroy.

Again, her life was anything but normal.

But for now at least, sitting at the café, she had to *look* ordinary. If not, someone might suspect that she was secretly keeping watch over the police station across the street. She stole another inconspicuous glance at the building.

"What do you see?" came a voice in her ear, courtesy of an Avengers earbud communication device, or comm. It was the voice of Steve Rogers, Captain America.

Wanda cast a casual glance over the guards

outside the station. "Standard guard team," she said aloud but quietly. "Small arms. Quiet street. It makes for a good target."

Cap responded, "There's an ATM on the south corner, which means—"

"Cameras," Wanda finished, spotting the ATM Steve was referring to. The camera pointed right at the door of the station.

"Both cross streets are one-way," said Cap, referring to the intersection where the police station sat.

"So the possible escape routes are compromised," Wanda concluded.

"That's right," said Cap.

Cap was set up in a second-floor hotel room across the street from the café where Wanda was sipping her tea. From his position at the window, he had a clear view of Wanda, the station, and most of the street. Several local newspapers were

scattered next to him on the hotel bed. One of the headlines read TERROR GROUP TARGETS POLICE.

"So this is what we know: Our guy doesn't care if he's caught on camera and isn't afraid of making a mess on the way out. Do you clock the SUV halfway down the block?"

From her chair in the café, Wanda turned slightly and eyeballed the vehicle Cap was talking about.

"Red one," she said. "It's cute."

"It's also bulletproof," said Natasha Romanoff, the spy known by the code name Black Widow, as she slipped into a chair at the table next to Wanda. "Meaning more private security. Meaning more guns and more headaches for somebody...probably us."

Wanda looked away from the SUV as a garbage truck pulled up, blocking her view. She made a face at Widow. Were the others really worried about a few more guys with firearms? "You know I can move things with my mind, right?" she asked Widow.

"Powers are great," said Widow. "But you still have to look over your shoulder. That needs to become second nature."

"The difference between that and paranoia is what?" came a new voice over the comms. Wanda looked up, recognizing the voice as belonging to Sam Wilson, a.k.a. Falcon, who was currently flying a watch patrol above their area in his wing suit.

"The difference doesn't matter—" Widow began.

"Eyes back on the target, folks," interrupted Cap. "We know Rumlow's been unstable since DC, so be ready."

Cap meant Brock Rumlow, a former S.H.I.E.L.D. agent Cap had run missions with. It turned out

that Rumlow was a deep-cover Hydra agent inside S.H.I.E.L.D. Rumlow had betrayed Cap and tried to kill him in an elevator, but Cap escaped.

Rumlow was there when a Helicarrier fell out of the sky and slammed into the S.H.I.E.L.D. base, but word was that he had made it out alive, though burned, and was now wearing a skull-like mask and working as a mercenary under the code name Crossbones.

Cap and his team had gone all the way to Africa to track down Rumlow. Reports had made their way to the Avengers Compound in upstate New York that Crossbones and his mercenary gang intended to hit this city block. Given the threats he'd made against law enforcement in the past, the station seemed like an obvious target. The attack could happen any minute.

Cap was still thinking about Rumlow when he

took a second look at a garbage truck. It was riding low, almost scraping the ground. Why would it be so heavy?

Cap called an order to Falcon. "Sam, Allen Street. Garbage truck. Check it out."

High above, perched on the edge of a downtown skyscraper, Sam signaled his drone, Redwing, which automatically deployed from its pack. The high-tech flying surveillance gear zoomed away, a silver-and-red jet-powered bird in the sky. "On it, Cap," said Falcon.

As the drone flew over the garbage truck, Falcon commanded it to take an X-ray scan of the truck and send the video feed wirelessly to Falcon's goggles. The images of the interior of the truck revealed a stack of cinder blocks and a group of men carrying heavy artillery weapons.

"That truck's loaded for weight, and the driver's armed," reported Falcon.

Suddenly, Widow realized what Crossbones's plan had to be. "That truck's a battering ram," she said.

Up in his hotel room, Cap looked over the map. It made no sense. The truck was pointing the wrong direction. It couldn't hit the police station the way it was headed. But...

"Everyone, go now!" Cap shouted.

"What's happening?" asked Wanda, suddenly frantic.

"They're not hitting the police station after all," Cap announced as he sprang into action.

Wanda, Widow, and Falcon all jumped up, realizing Cap was right. The police station had been a distraction!

They raced forward, watching as the garbage truck smashed head-on into a different building. Wanda looked up, reading the sign on the building. THE INSTITUTE FOR INFECTIOUS DISEASE.

The bored and distracted guards at Lagos's Institute for Infectious Disease were used to uneventful shifts. Even though the institute's vaults held deadly biological and chemical agents, no one had ever actually attempted to break in. Because of that, a guard shift usually consisted of talking about soccer with fellow guards, playing cards, or checking out old movies on the TV in the security office.

That's why all the guards were taken by utter surprise when Crossbones's truck crashed right into the front gates of the institute.

By the time the shocked guards pulled out their weapons and ran into the courtyard, the truck had already screeched to a halt and armed mercenaries were swarming the building.

The guards were clearly outnumbered, but they still tried to defend their posts. Then the mercenaries pulled gas masks over their faces and fired smoke canisters. Soon smoke filled every corner of the courtyard and most of the institute building. The guards had no choice but to flee, leaving the building to the attackers.

Several masked mercenaries marched confidently into the building, heading right for a laboratory protected by a thick glass barrier. Inside

that lab was the object they had been hired to acquire.

One of the mercenaries opened fire on the barrier with his machine gun, but the glass barely even cracked. It was bulletproof. How were they going to get in?

"Move, idiot," said someone behind them.

The mercenaries turned to see their boss, Crossbones, complete with his skull mask, stepping forward through the smoke.

Crossbones pressed a button on the huge gloves he wore and they powered up. They were called hydraulic gauntlets and they enhanced his punches, making them ten times stronger. Once they were at full power, Crossbones pounded on the glass, shattering it instantly!

Soon Crossbones and his men were inside the lab, grabbing what they'd gone there for. It was a test tube filled with a very dangerous virus.

The virus was so contagious that if it got into the wrong hands, it could be used as a deadly weapon to infect millions of people.

Outside, one of Crossbones's mercenaries was guarding the steps from the courtyard into the building. That was until Falcon streaked down out of the sky and slammed into him like a 250-pound cannonball!

Behind the mercs, Cap jumped onto the back of the crashed truck and knocked out another operative. "I make eight hostiles," Cap said into his comm.

Sam, proving he deserved the code name Falcon, shot into the air, firing a grappling hook at one of the mercenaries on the roof and dragging him away. Then he flew across the roof and took out two more.

"Count again," said Sam. "Now there are only five!"

Near Falcon, Scarlet Witch descended from the sky, projecting red energy against the ground to keep herself aloft. Unsure of herself, she landed, half stumbling. When one of the mercenaries saw her, he opened fire!

But Wanda used one hand to expel energy that bent his bullets away from her, and used the other hand to telekinetically draw the mercenary toward her, then lift him into the air.

"Sam!" she shouted as she threw the combatant upward.

"On it," said Sam, swooping low and clotheslining the thug with his wing.

"We need eyes!" shouted Cap.

"Redwing, deploy," said Sam. On cue, his small drone launched from its wing pack. The drone rose quickly above the scene, shooting live video that it sent straight back to a digital display inside Sam's flight goggles. Sam could see everything Redwing saw.

"We've got movement on the third floor," said Sam, watching Redwing's feed.

From the third floor, a man fired an automatic rifle at Sam, but Sam closed his wings, using them to deflect the bullets. Then he launched a missile from his wing suit, taking out the section of the building where the shots had come from.

"We're down to three," Sam noted.

Cap approached Wanda. "Let's do this like we practiced," he said.

"What about the gas?" asked Wanda.

"Get rid of it," Cap instructed.

Cap climbed up on a jeep's hood, then used it

to launch himself into the air. As soon as he was off the ground, Wanda performed the same move they'd been practicing over and over again in the Avengers Compound training room. She used her powers to give Cap a big telekinetic push, and he flew up through the hole that Sam's missile had just created in the third floor.

The two mercenaries who were inside the third-floor room were shocked to see Cap. As Cap knocked them out, Wanda used her abilities to drain the gas from the building and vent it up into the sky.

Hearing the sounds of combat, Crossbones knew the Avengers had arrived and that it was time for him to go. Busting through the building's far wall, Crossbones looked out and down at his getaway trucks. He and his men shot zip lines and quickly slid down to their vehicles.

The trucks took off just as Cap ran into the vault and saw that it had been ransacked.

"Crossbones has the bio agent," Cap reported to the others through his comm.

"On it," Black Widow responded.

Down on the street, Black Widow gunned the engine on her motorcycle and caught up to Crossbones's getaway truck. Without missing a beat she leaped from the bike and flipped onto the roof of the truck, where she started knocking out bad guy after bad guy as they climbed onto the roof to fight her.

But Black Widow was so busy with the others,

she didn't realize that Crossbones himself had ascended to the roof and was standing right behind her. Once she saw him, she fired one of her electrical Widow's Bite darts from the gauntlet on her wrist...but it had no effect.

"Those don't work on me anymore. Sorry," said Crossbones.

Crossbones took Widow down, dropping her through a hatch into the back of the truck. Then he pitched in a grenade after her.

Natasha landed next to two mercenaries, who were surprised to see her but even more surprised that their boss had just thrown an explosive at them! Natasha and the mercenaries all scrambled to leap out of the truck before the grenade detonated.

Natasha landed hard on the ground and rolled to safety, hearing the blast behind her.

Crossbones climbed into the cab of another truck, then looked up. He saw Sam streaking toward him in his wing suit.

"We're not going to outrun them. Hit the market. We'll try to lose them in the crowd," Crossbones instructed his driver.

Crossbones turned to one of the mercenaries and handed off the test tube.

"Get this to the airstrip," he commanded.

As the truck pulled into a busy street market crowded with people, Crossbones explained his plan to the remaining men. They were all to take off in different directions. One of them had the virus, but the others would act as decoys, dividing the Avengers' attention.

"Let's go!" Crossbones shouted.

Sam, Natasha, and Cap all reached the market at about the same time and saw Crossbones's men running into the crowd.

"Spread out. Find which one really has the payload," Cap shouted over the comms.

Suddenly, Cap heard a loud *thunk* and felt an impact as a magnetic grenade slammed into his shield and stuck there! Knowing he had seconds before the explosive went off, Cap hurled his shield into the air.

The grenade detonated harmlessly, away from Cap and anyone else, but it left Cap without his shield...exactly as Crossbones wanted.

Crossbones leaped down, landing next to Cap and hitting him with the full force of his hydraulic gauntlets. Without his shield as defense, and without time to react, Cap was forced to withstand blow after punishing blow from the mechanically assisted punches!

Not far from Cap, the escaping mercenaries were weaving through the crowd, dodging the other Avengers. The soldiers were pulling off their armor plates and other gear to reveal their civilian clothes underneath. They hoped they would soon blend in with everyone else in the busy market.

Sam used his wing suit to swoop low over the crowd, scanning for his targets. Finally spotting one, Sam dove down, shoved the villain into a stall, and grabbed his bag. But when he opened it, nothing was inside. It was clearly one of the decoys.

Falcon radioed Black Widow: "I'm empty here."

Natasha got the message just as she was vaulting over a table filled with sale items, chasing another one of the mercenaries. She ran up the side of one wall, took a huge leap, and landed right in front of the man she was after.

The mercenary jumped back in surprise as Natasha pointed her weapon at him and nodded toward his bag. "Pick up any nice souvenirs?" she asked.

The mercenary went pale...but then he looked at something over Natasha's shoulder and started to smile. Natasha spun around to see a second mercenary behind her...and in his hand was the virus test tube.

"Drop it," the man said, indicating Natasha's weapon, "or I drop this."

Natasha considered her options. If the virus

was released in the busy marketplace, it could easily spread across the country and maybe even the globe. But if she let the criminals escape with it, they could use it any time or place they wanted.

Fortunately, it wasn't a decision she had to make.

BAM! The mercenary with the virus was hit by a laser strike from behind. He dropped the test tube as he fell, but Natasha leaped forward and caught it.

She looked up to see Sam's Redwing drone hovering nearby. It had pulled off a great shot.

"Payload secure," Natasha reported. "Thanks, Sam."

Looking at the virtual display in his goggles, Sam could see Natasha through the drone's camera. "And you thought I was wasting my money with this thing," he teased her.

Crossbones kept hammering Cap with his hydraulic gauntlets, but Cap picked his moment carefully and dove at Crossbones, in a split second spinning him around and slamming him into a nearby wall. The impact shattered Crossbones's skull mask, revealing a deeply twisted and scarred face.

Crossbones saw Cap's reaction to his appearance and joked, "I think I look pretty good, all things considered."

"Where are the weapons?" Cap demanded.

"I'm a dancing monkey, Rogers. Just like you," Crossbones replied with a twisted smile. "Whoever pays me plays me."

Lunging forward, Crossbones tried to bite Cap, but Cap sidestepped him easily.

"You know, he knew you," taunted Crossbones.

"What did you say?"

"Your pal. Your buddy. Your Bucky. He remembers you," said Crossbones, satisfied by the disturbed look his words brought to Cap's face. "I was there. He got all weepy about it."

Cap realized that Crossbones was talking about James "Bucky" Barnes, Cap's best friend. Bucky had been a good man, but Hydra brainwashed him, turning him into a deadly assassin with some of the same enhanced physical abilities Cap possessed.

Cap wanted desperately to find his friend and help him. Because of that, Cap drew closer to Crossbones, not realizing how much he was letting his guard down.

Crossbones continued, lowering the volume of his voice to draw Cap even closer to him: "He wanted you to know something. He said to me,

'Please tell him, please tell Rogers...when you gotta go, you gotta go!'"

With Cap now very close to him, Crossbones pressed a button in his hand. Hearing the clicking of the button, Cap looked down and realized that Crossbones had triggered an explosive in his vest!

Cap covered himself defensively as the device went off, bracing for the force of the blast.

But he felt nothing.

He looked up to see that the explosion had suddenly stopped! It hovered in the air as a perfectly round ball of fire, as if it were frozen in time!

Just behind him, Wanda stepped out. She was using her supernatural powers to control the explosion.

"I...I can't—can't hold it!" Wanda said, visibly straining with the mental effort of containing the blast.

Suddenly, she dropped to her knees and used

all the energy she had left to hurl the fireball into the air, away from the crowded market streets.

But because Wanda had used up the last of her power, as the blast flew away, it resumed its violent expansion.

The force of the explosion was so strong that it ripped into the seventh floor of a nearby hotel. Glass and debris flew everywhere.

Cap didn't miss a beat. "We need fire and rescue to the north side of the building!" he shouted into his comm.

Cap ran into the building, trying to help.

Wanda stared at the destruction, tears welling in her eyes.

CHAPTER 3

In a large theater on the campus of Tony Stark's alma mater, a packed audience watched as a giant screen showed video from an old home movie. In the video a beautiful middle-aged woman named Maria Stark played the piano. The camera got closer to her, and from behind the camera came the voice of a young Tony Stark.

"I'm going to send this tape to *Star Search*," he said.

Maria just giggled. Then, from the hallway, another voice: "Maria, have you seen my golf shoes?" Into the frame of the video stepped Howard Stark, dressed in garish golf clothes—green pants and a pink shirt.

"Hi, Dad," said young Tony. "First day at Clown College?"

Howard pulled a pained face. "Why aren't you at work?"

"I'm taking some time," explained Tony. "Dr. Klein says it's essential for my emotional development."

Howard sighed. "I swear I pay that man to undermine me."

"Try looking on the top shelf in the garage," said Maria.

As Howard scooted off to check the garage,

young Tony walked the camera closer to Maria. Tony sat down next to his mother on the piano bench. His mom kissed him on the cheek and then pointed at the piano. "Come on, let's play together like we used to—"

At that moment, the video cut to static—and then the opening credits of an eighties action TV show appeared on-screen.

"I guess I really needed to see that episode," the real-life Tony Stark said, looking up as the show's theme played on. The video cut off, and the lights went up. Tony kept talking to the crowd. "Beyond my love of period haircuts, I show this to make a point. Life is an omnisensory whirlwind, and our best whack at preserving it is this?"

Emotion had crept into Tony's voice, and he stopped a moment to compose himself before continuing. "I've watched that tape a thousand times since the incident—since my parents died. But it's not enough. I don't want to just see my mom. I want to smell her coffee, feel the sunlight coming in the windows. I want to feel my dad's footsteps coming back after he finds out his shoes weren't in the garage after all. I want to be able to show that to you, and make you feel it... but that kind of technology is impossible."

Looking out at the crowd, Tony paused, trying to connect with his audience. "At least, it's impossible *in my lifetime* ... but not in yours."

Tony made a gesture and a spotlight turned on, shining onto the first four rows of seats. The students looked around, confused, trying to figure out why the lights were on them. Tony spoke directly to them.

"You kids are the pick of the brain crop," he said. "Physicists, engineers, scientists... nothing in common with one another except a desire to innovate, and the fact that not one of you has a dime." Everyone chuckled at that.

"Well, that changes today," Tony continued. He pointed up at the blank screen. "AV department, can I get a little 'zazz?'"

On cue, the screen blinked to life, showing a picture of Tony's parents and a logo that read THE HOWARD AND MARIA STARK FOUNDATION.

"You are all the recipients of the inaugural Howard and Maria Stark Foundation grant," said Tony to the students. "Every one of your projects is approved and funded. No strings, no taxes. All you have to do is invent the future…starting *now*!"

The audience erupted in applause.

Backstage after the press conference, a university representative approached Tony. "If you've got a second, we've got some alums who'd kill for a picture."

Tony peered over the rep's shoulder and saw a crowd of university donors looking anxious to talk to him.

"I'd love to," Tony said in a tone that didn't make it sound like he'd love to at all.

Then he turned and saw a woman in her forties standing in the corridor, looking at him.

"It was nice, what you did for those young people," said the woman.

"Thank you," Tony said, taken aback by the emotion in the woman's eyes.

"It must ease your conscience," she continued, her voice growing harder. "Do you even know how many people you've killed?"

Suddenly on alert, Tony flicked his eyes around the room. The woman was standing between him and the door. There were no security cameras in the corridor. "You're not on the alumni committee, are you?" he asked.

The woman started to reach into her purse, but Tony instinctively grabbed her hand, stopping her in case she was going for a weapon. But the withering look she gave him—as if to say, *Of course you would think that*—caused Tony to release her hand.

Instead of a weapon, she pulled out a photo of a handsome teenage boy and offered it to Tony.

"Who is he?" Tony asked, taking the picture.

"My son," said the woman. "You killed him."

Tony was stunned. A thick silence hung in the air for a moment.

"His name is Damien," the woman continued. "He was killed in Sokovia, crushed by a building that your friends and your robots knocked down. As if that matters to you in the slightest."

"No, listen, it does. It matters," Tony said urgently.

But the woman wasn't listening. "You hide behind your money and your ego. You pat yourself on the back and bestow your greatness upon us. But no one can hold you accountable. My son is dead, and you're being honored?" She shook her head, as if unable to believe what the world had come to. "I don't honor you, Tony Stark. I blame you. I wanted you to know that."

The woman turned to go. All Tony could muster was a quiet "I'm sorry."

She looked at him over her shoulder. "That's not going to bring him back," she said. And then she was gone, leaving the photo in Tony's hand.

Wanda sat alone in her room at the Avengers Compound, watching a news report about the aftermath of the Avengers' mission in Nigeria.

It had not ended well.

When Crossbones and his mercenary crew had scattered, the team split up, trying to catch whoever had the virus-filled vial. Cap stuck to Crossbones. The mercenary gave Cap a run for his money, but in the end Cap had him trapped, cornered.

It should have ended there, with a clean capture and the virus recovered.

But it didn't.

Crossbones had been wired with explosives. He initiated a blast that would have taken out Cap and many innocent bystanders. Seeing that, Scarlet Witch, Black Widow, and Falcon jumped into action. Wanda planned to use her powers to levitate the explosives away from the scene and send them high into the sky.

But Wanda didn't have enough strength to contain them and the explosives went off only a few stories above the street, destroying a huge section of the adjacent hotel.

Wanda watched the aftermath of the destruction on a news report. "Eleven Wakandans were amongst those killed in the Nigerian hotel explosion that—"

Suddenly, the TV shut off. Wanda turned to see Steve in the doorway, holding the remote. They shared a look.

"It's our fault," said Wanda. Even with the TV off, the images of the devastated block of downtown Lagos played in her mind. "Why couldn't we have responded sooner, gotten the explosives away from people in time?"

"I don't see it as our fault," said Cap.

"Turn the TV back on. They were being very specific."

"I should have seen that bomb vest before any

of you had to deal with it," said Cap. "And people died because of that. It's on me."

He searched a moment for the right words before continuing. "In this job we try to save as many as we can. Sometimes that doesn't mean all of them. If you don't find a way to live with that…then next time, maybe nobody gets saved."

As Wanda considered Cap's words, a ghostly face suddenly emerged from her wall.

Startled, Wanda shouted in surprise before realizing it was only Vision, the android Avenger. He had the power to phase through solid matter, as if walls were just curtains of fog.

"Please accept my apologies, Wanda," said Vision, his body moving fully into the room. The robot really seemed sorry to have scared her. "Captain Rogers wanted to know when Mr. Stark was arriving," he explained.

Cap nodded his thanks to Vision. "I'll be right down."

Vision continued, "It appears Mr. Stark brought a guest."

"Do we know who?" asked Cap.

"The US secretary of state," Vision replied matter-of-factly.

CHAPTER 4

General Thaddeus E. Ross had traded his uniform for a conservative blue suit. Long before, while still active in the military, Ross had been involved in the experiment that turned Bruce Banner into the Hulk. For many years after, Ross had devoted his time and energy to hunting down the Hulk, but with no success.

As US secretary of state, Ross was older and

calmer, less of a warrior and more of a politician. But those early experiences with the Hulk had colored Ross's view of enhanced individuals... like the ones he was facing right now.

"While many see you as heroes," Ross said, addressing the group in front of him, "others would use the word *vigilantes*."

"What word would you use?" Steve asked Ross.

With the full team assembled in the Avengers Compound's conference room, Tony Stark, Sam Wilson, Natasha Romanoff, Wanda Maximoff, James "Rhodey" Rhodes, and Vision all watched as Ross diplomatically responded to Steve's question.

"How about *headache*?" Ross said. "What would you call a group of US-based enhanced combatants who ignore sovereign borders and inflict their will anywhere in the world?"

Ross's response caused many of the Avengers to exchange wounded looks.

Ross continued. "Since 2008 the US government has had to hold its feet to the fire because of you. The president is reluctant to act, but recent events have made ignoring this issue impossible."

Ross pressed a button, and images of destruction appeared on the room's holo-display. "New York...Washington, DC...Sokovia...Johannesburg...Lagos..." listed Ross as he presented photos of each war-torn location.

Steve saw Wanda shiver as she looked at the hologram of Lagos, hovering like a ghost in front of her. "That's enough," Steve said sharply.

Ross complied, shutting off the holo-display but looking Steve in the eyes. "Right now you operate with unlimited power and no supervision. That's an arrangement that the governments of the world can no longer tolerate...but I think we've come up with a solution."

Ross produced a thick document, placing it on the table in front of the Avengers. "The Sokovia Accords. Approved by one hundred and seventeen countries. It states that the Avengers shall no longer be a private organization. Instead, they will operate under the supervision of a panel. You'll act only when and if the panel deems it necessary."

The Avengers were stunned.

"You'll forgive us if we're feeling a little blindsided here," Natasha managed to say.

"That's only because you haven't been paying attention," Ross replied, his voice grave. "People are afraid."

"The whole reason the Avengers were formed was to make the world a safer place," Steve pointed out.

"Tell me, Cap," said Ross, "do you know where Thor and Banner are right now?"

Cap looked at Ross, refusing to reply.

Ross continued, "If I'd misplaced a couple of thirty-megaton nukes, you can bet there'd be consequences." Then he pointed at Vision and Wanda. "And what about these two? Do you even know the extent of what they can do?"

Vision stepped in. "Ms. Maximoff manipulates molecular polarity, allowing her to alter physical reality...but I'm a little harder to explain."

"And you're not the only ones. More enhanced beings pop up every day." Ross addressed the whole room, pointing at the document on the table. "Compromise. Reassurance. That's the way the world keeps working. Believe me. This is the middle ground."

Ross looked around at the faces of the Avengers. Each member was clearly thinking hard about what he had just said. He turned to leave.

"In three days they meet in Vienna to ratify the Sokovia Accords. Talk it over."

"And if we don't come to a decision you like?" asked Natasha.

Ross raised an eyebrow. "Then you retire."

With that, he walked out of the room.

An hour later the Avengers were still sitting there, discussing the accords. The conference room was littered with empty water bottles and half-drunk cups of coffee.

"It's not like you don't take orders now," said Rhodey to Sam, continuing the debate.

"I take orders from him," said Sam, pointing at Cap. "Because he earned it. He didn't walk into my living room and demand it."

"There's nothing wrong with a chain of command," said Rhodey.

"Says the lieutenant colonel at the top of the chain," snorted Sam.

"Actually, I'm a full colonel now," Rhodey replied.

Vision shook his head. "You're undercutting your argument," he pointed out.

Sam slapped his hand down on the copy of the accords. "Say we sign these. How long until we're LoJacked like a bunch of convicts?"

Natasha looked at him. "Now who's being paranoid?"

"During hurricane season, they evacuated my mom and sister immediately. Coordinated government authority," said Rhodey. "It kind of works."

Cap shook his head. "Hurricanes can be predicted. The kind of things we deal with can't."

Vision stood up. "I have an equation," he said.

"Oh, this will clear things up," said Sam sarcastically.

Vision activated the holo-display and a graph filled the air in front of him.

"In the eight years since Tony Stark announced himself as Iron Man, the number of enhanced persons has grown exponentially. The number of potentially world-ending events has grown at a commiserative rate."

Rhodey frowned. "You're saying this is our fault?"

"No," said Vision, "but there may be causality. Our strength invites challenge. Challenge incites conflict. Conflict breeds catastrophe.... Oversight is not an idea that should be dismissed out of hand."

Tony studied Vision's graph, and Natasha realized that in all the debating, Tony had yet to weigh in. "You're being uncharacteristically non-hyperverbal," she remarked to him dryly.

Cap spoke up. "That's because he's already made up his mind."

The rest of the Avengers turned to look at Tony Stark.

He pulled a crumpled photo out of his pocket— the one the woman had given him backstage. He showed it to the room.

"Damien Sharpe. Good-looking kid. Graduated from college, took off for Europe. Did it right, hit all the hotspots. London, Paris, Rome— then he stopped off in Sokovia."

Wanda closed her eyes, realizing where Tony was going.

"He was helping evacuate the hotel where he was staying. And the ceiling fell in on him. He died. Probably not instantly, but he wasn't the only one."

Tony looked at his team solemnly.

"I've made a lot of mistakes," he said. "If agreeing to some tiny measure of parental guidance will let people sleep at night...then I don't see a choice here."

Cap looked at Damien's picture for a long moment before finally saying, "Someone dies on your watch, you don't give up."

Tony frowned. "We're not giving up."

"We are if we're not responsible for our actions," said Cap.

Rhodey felt his frustration building. "This isn't S.H.I.E.L.D. It's not the World Security Council. It's not Hydra—"

"No," said Cap, interrupting. "But it's run by people with an agenda. And agendas change."

"That's a good thing," said Tony. "When I found out what my weapons were doing to people, I stopped making them."

Cap sighed. "You chose to do that. We sign this and we surrender our right to choose. That's why I enlisted. That's why I spent seventy years in the ice—for the freedom to choose. What if the panel sends us somewhere we don't want to go? What if there's somewhere we need to go and they won't let us?"

Cap looked over the Avengers...his teammates...his friends.

"I'm not saying we're perfect," he concluded, "but the safest hands are ours."

"Steve, listen to me," said Tony. "If we don't do this now, it will be done to us later." He glanced at Wanda. "And it won't be pretty."

Wanda returned his look. "You're saying they'll come for me."

Vision took a step toward her. "We would protect you."

Natasha cut in. "Maybe digging in our heels

isn't the best way to go about this. Maybe Tony is right."

Cap shot her a look of pure disappointment. "I have to go," he said. He left the Avengers Compound, not telling anyone where he was going.

A full day later, Cap still hadn't reported in. Natasha went out looking for him and found him alone in an old church, deep in thought. She sat in the pew next to him. They were the only two people in the little chapel.

Cap didn't even look up. They sat together for a long time before Natasha finally broke the silence. "I'm headed to Vienna for the accords ceremony."

Cap looked up at her, searching for something behind her eyes. "Who else signed?" he asked.

"Tony, Rhodey, and Vision."

"Clint?"

"He says he's retired."

"Wanda?"

"Not yet....Come with me. We can make this work."

Cap shook his head. "I can't."

"Staying together is more important than how we stay together."

Cap looked down. "But what are we giving up to do it?"

Natasha studied Cap's expression of resolve. Finally, she said, "In Russia, in the Red Room, there were dozens of us. All girls, all young. We lived together. They let us be friends. Then they dropped us in the tundra, two weeks' walk from home, with just enough supplies for one of us to survive."

Cap looked at her, understanding her meaning.

"Don't let them push us into the cold," she said.

"Natasha, I know what we mean to you. I do," said Cap softly. "You mean the same to me...."

Natasha smiled at that.

"But I'm sorry. I'm out."

CHAPTER 5

The complex in Vienna was mostly glass, symbolic of the transparency with which the panel promised to operate in regard to the citizens of the world. See-through walls suited Natasha Romanoff, who was concerned about security for the event.

The ratification of the Sokovia Accords, a controversial and influential document, was a potential draw for terrorists and criminals looking for an opportunity to strike multiple heads of state at the same time. Anyone of importance was there. And a number of organizations would benefit from the chaos that would ensue if the ratification day ceremony was attacked.

Natasha scanned the crowd, noticing nothing out of order so far. She watched as the delegates entered, shook hands, and made their way to their assigned areas.

In one corner she noticed T'Challa, the prince of Wakanda and son of King T'Chaka. The African country of Wakanda was abundant in vibranium, because a meteorite of the rare vibration-absorbing metal had crashed there. Furthermore, some of those who were killed in the Lagos incident were visiting Wakandan citizens and aid workers. Because of those two things, T'Challa's was a face Natasha was very familiar with.

She turned to scan the rest of the room, but when she turned back, T'Challa was gone. Natasha was just wondering where he had gone when she heard his voice over her shoulder.

"I suppose neither of us are comfortable in the spotlight," T'Challa said.

How had he been able to cross the room so quickly without her noticing? Natasha was surprised and slightly unnerved, but she tried not to let it show.

"Well, the spotlight isn't always flattering," she responded.

"You're doing all right so far," said T'Challa, offering Natasha a warm smile. He, too, turned to survey the growing crowd of delegates. "Given your last trip to Capitol Hill, I wouldn't think you'd be particularly comfortable in this company."

"I'm not."

"That alone makes me glad you're here, Ms. Romanoff."

"So," said Natasha, trying to size him up, "you don't approve of this?"

T'Challa cocked his head to the side, as if searching for a way to explain. "The accords, yes. The politics? Not really. Two people in a room can get more done than hundreds—"

"Unless you need to move a piano," someone interrupted. Natasha and T'Challa both turned to find T'Challa's father, T'Chaka, standing right behind them.

Natasha frowned. First T'Challa had managed to sneak up on her—the Black Widow—and now his father, too. What *was* it with that family?

The king extended a hand to Natasha. "Ms. Romanoff," he said, by way of greeting.

Natasha shook the monarch's hand. "King T'Chaka, allow me to personally extend the Avengers' condolences for what happened in Nigeria."

"Thank you," responded the king. "And thank

you for agreeing to all of this. I know power is not easily shared."

"It's never been about power for us," Natasha assured him.

"Yet you'd be unable to act without it," the king said. "I'm sad to hear that Captain Rogers won't be joining us today."

Natasha smiled awkwardly. "So am I."

Somewhere in the hall a bell chimed, inviting the delegates to take their seats.

"That's the future calling, Ms. Romanoff," said T'Challa. "After you." He bowed, letting Natasha walk down the aisle ahead of him.

Before T'Challa could follow her, T'Chaka put a hand on his shoulder, stopping him. "For a man who disapproves of diplomacy, you're getting good at it," he said to his son.

"I have nothing against diplomacy," T'Challa replied. "Only diplomats."

King T'Chaka stood at the podium, giving the keynote speech to the assembled body. "I'm thankful to the Avengers for supporting this initiative," he said, then continued his remarks.

Natasha was only half listening. She'd heard enough speeches and knew enough about government affairs that she could predict every word. Instead, she devoted the majority of her attention to scanning for potential threats. When she saw T'Challa notice something through the glass walls of the building, she followed his gaze—and then she saw it, too.

There was a commotion surrounding a van parked on the street in front of the building. Security guards were running around it—some toward it, others away from it…

Instinctively, Natasha grabbed the delegates that were closest to her and yanked them under the protection of the table, just as a bomb went off!

The massive explosion sent people flying through the air. The glass walls of the complex shattered, throwing a curtain of shards all over the room.

T'Challa jumped to his father's side, pulling him down to shield him from the projectiles—too late. His father was hit....

Back in the United States, Steve was sitting in a hotel room with Sam Wilson and his friend Sharon Carter.

Sharon, also known as Agent 13, was once an undercover S.H.I.E.L.D. liaison assigned to live in an apartment near Cap and report on all his activities. She proved to be a helpful ally during the fall of S.H.I.E.L.D., and they'd since become good friends. Sharon now worked for a security task force run by an international authority.

The three friends were enjoying one another's company until a news report broke in, showing images of the destruction in Vienna. They saw the shattered glass, the destroyed building, the injured being loaded into ambulances...

The recording of an interview with Tony Stark played over the footage. "Today was an atrocity," Tony said, choking back emotion, "and the Avengers stand ready to assist in any way that we are asked."

Then the news played CCTV footage of the person who was seen setting the bomb. Cap looked closely.... *It couldn't be!* But it was.

The image showed Bucky Barnes.

Bucky and Cap had grown up on the same

block in Brooklyn in the 1930s and played together as children. When America entered World War II, Bucky and the then-superpowered Cap got the chance to serve together. Bucky was a member of the elite Howling Commandos unit, fighting alongside Cap. As childhood friends and also brothers-in-arms, Cap and Bucky were as close as two friends could be.

But during combat against the villainous Red Skull, Bucky had been lost. Cap had believed his best friend dead. Then Cap was lost, too, frozen in Arctic ice.

When Cap's body was discovered and miraculously thawed out in the present-day world, he believed everyone he had ever known was gone. He thought he was alone.

Only recently had Cap discovered that Bucky had been kept alive and brainwashed by Arnim Zola—a Hydra scientist who had worked with

Red Skull and infiltrated S.H.I.E.L.D. Zola had turned Bucky into a living weapon for Hydra, and Cap's old friend had become an unwilling terrorist pawn, known by the code name the Winter Soldier.

Sam and Sharon saw the footage, too, and knew what it would mean to Cap. Sharon got a text on her phone, which brought Steve out of his reverie. Looking at it, she said, "I have to go to work."

Within thirty minutes she was on a military plane headed for Vienna.

Standing at the blast site, Natasha surveyed the damage. Half the building had been torn away. Hundreds of people had been injured. It was another chaotic situation. She noticed Sharon had arrived on the scene and was running intel from a makeshift work tent. She also saw T'Challa picking his way through the wreckage.

Natasha approached T'Challa, who seemed lost in thought. He was covered in dust from the blast and looked upset.

The prince's face grew hard, which worried Natasha. Then she glanced over as he picked up a printout that showed Bucky Barnes, the Winter Soldier, walking away from the bomb van. He stared at the image, intensity in his eyes. Natasha looked from T'Challa's face to the picture. She knew he was upset and would try to hunt down the Winter Soldier to avenge the lives lost in the bombing.

"T'Challa, the authorities will decide who brings in Bucky Barnes."

"Tell them not to bother, Ms. Romanoff," T'Challa said casually. "I'll take care of him myself."

Natasha watched him walk away.

She could tell it wasn't going to end well.

The moment Steve's cell phone rang, he knew who it would be. "Are you all right?" he asked, truly concerned.

"I got lucky," Natasha replied. "So you already know?"

"Yeah."

There was silence on the line for a second as Natasha collected her thoughts.

"I have to warn you away," she said finally. "This is how it works now. I know what Barnes means to you. But stay home. You'll only make things worse for all of us."

Steve raised an eyebrow. "Are you saying you'd arrest me?"

"Someone will," she replied, "if you interfere."

Steve softened. "Natasha, if he's this far gone, I need to be the one to bring him in."

"Why?"

"Because I'm the one least likely to die trying."

"Steve…" Natasha started, a note of concern creeping into her voice.

But Steve hung up and looked out across the plaza in front of the international complex.

He was already in Vienna.

From the patio of the café across the street he couldn't see *everything*, but he could eyeball the blast radius, which allowed him to estimate the yield of the bomb. There were only a few classes of conventional explosives that could pack the punch necessary to do that level of damage.

Next he spotted Sharon, hustling back and forth with reports, taking the lead in straightening out the investigation.

Cap ducked through the doorframe into the little café, where he found Sam Wilson at the espresso bar, eating an Austrian torte. Sam had seen Cap hang up the phone.

"She tell you to stay out of it?" he asked. When Cap nodded, Sam continued. "She might have had a point."

"He'd do it for me," said Cap, remembering how close he and Bucky had been.

"In 1945 maybe," Sam replied.

Cap shot him a look.

Sam held up a hand, as if to ward off Cap's glare. "Hey," he said defensively, "I just like to know we've considered all the options. The people who shoot at you usually wind up shooting at me."

At that moment, Sharon stepped up to the bar. She looked straight ahead, not acknowledging Steve or Sam. They did the same. To any casual outside observers, it would seem like the woman was a stranger to the two men.

"Tips have been pouring in since that photo went public," Sharon said under her breath, still not looking in Cap's direction. "Everybody thinks that Winter Soldier goes to their gym. Most of it's noise, except for this...." Sharon set an open file on the bar in front of her.

Cap leaned over casually and glanced at the page.

Sharon continued. "My boss expects a briefing"—she checked her watch—"pretty much now. So this is all the head start you get."

Natasha Romanoff, a.k.a. Black Widow, must stop the theft of volatile chemicals from a Nigerian lab.

Thankfully, she's not alone. She has the help of Sam Wilson, a.k.a. the Falcon...

...and Steve Rogers. Captain America is the original Super-Soldier, the first Avenger, and a former S.H.I.E.L.D. operative.

Former Hydra agent Brock Rumlow is now operating as Crossbones. He comes out of the lab looking to fight...

...but the brawl doesn't end well for him. Captain America brings him to justice.

Soon after, the Avengers are forced to discuss their place in the world. Steve believes that they have to be independent and free to act in everyone's best interests.

Not everyone agrees. Tony Stark, a.k.a. Iron Man, thinks the Avengers should be responsible for damages caused by their super-powered fights, and be accoutable to authorities.

Meanwhile, across the world, Bucky Barnes—Steve's best friend, who became the Winter Soldier after being brainwashed—is being hunted by a shadowy newcomer.

Falcon has been helping Captain America find Bucky, with the hope that they can help him overcome his brainwashing before it's too late.

Now Captain America is torn—will he help his friend, or fall in line with the law?

Captain America chooses to surrender for now...but he's convinced there's a conspiracy behind recent events—and the divide between the Avengers.

Cap nodded, grateful for the minimal intelligence she had to share. "Thanks," he added.

"One other thing," she said. "You're going to have to hurry. GSG9 is also on the way. They have orders to shoot to kill."

Sharon walked out without another word.

James Buchanan "Bucky" Barnes walked through a street market in Bucharest, Romania, checking out the vibrant fruit stalls. In the reflection of a building, he noticed a man watching him from across the street. But as Bucky approached him, the man sprinted away, leaving behind the newspaper he'd been reading. Bucky grabbed the newspaper and, to his surprise, saw photos of himself—the Winter Soldier. According to the information in the newspaper, Bucky was being accused of the bombing in Vienna.

Shocked, Bucky stumbled backward. He was disappointed, too. He had liked Romania, and now he had to leave behind another home—and fast.

Cap entered the shabby studio apartment and looked around. It was tiny and contained only a broken sofa and unmade bed. Scanning the room, Cap noticed the fridge was unplugged. He walked over to it and pulled open the door. Inside, instead of leftovers, were racks and racks of weapons and ammo.

"GSG9 is approaching from the south," Sam said via the comms. The GSG9 was a German military task force, one of the best tactical units in the world.

"Understood," Cap said.

Cap moved to the kitchen table, which held stacks of notebooks. He opened one and looked inside. There were hastily sketched maps and illustrations, random words written in an almost unreadable scrawl. It looked like the efforts of a distorted mind spilled across the pages.

Then Cap heard a footfall. He turned to see Bucky standing outside the apartment's open window.

The two old friends stared at each other for a beat.

"Do you know me?" Cap asked.

"You're Steve," Bucky said.

Encouraged, Cap took a step forward, but Bucky took a step back.

"I read about you in a museum," Bucky hastily added.

Sam spoke to Cap again over the comms: "They've set the perimeter."

"I know you're nervous, and you've got plenty of reasons to be," Cap said to Bucky. Then he studied his friend's face. "But you're lying," he concluded. Bucky didn't remember him; Cap could tell by the look in his eyes.

"I wasn't in Vienna," Bucky said simply. "I don't do that anymore."

Cap nodded toward the fridge. "But you like to stay ready."

"I have plenty of reasons to be nervous," said Bucky, using Cap's own words.

"People who think you were the reason for what happened in Vienna are coming right now, and they're not planning on taking you alive."

"That's smart," acknowledged Bucky. "Good strategy."

Falcon broke in over the comms. "They're on the roof. Overwatch is compromised."

Cap heard Sam but kept talking to Bucky. "This doesn't have to end in a fight," he said.

Cap took another step toward Bucky. Bucky flinched.

"Five seconds," Sam warned in Cap's ear.

"You pulled me out of the river," Cap said to Bucky, calling back to the moment amid the chaos of the Washington, DC, incident when Bucky had saved Cap from drowning.

"I don't know why I did that," Bucky said, shaking his head.

"Three seconds," came Sam's voice, starting to sound desperate.

"Yes, you do," said Cap, looking Bucky in the eyes.

"BREACH! BREACH! BREACH!" Falcon shouted as several GSG9 troops busted into the apartment.

"Get down, get down!" the troops yelled at Cap.

Bucky's reaction was automatic, seemingly programmed. He leaped forward, used Cap's shield to deflect GSG9's cover fire, and then pounded his metal fist into the floor. He lifted out an escape bag he had stored there for such an emergency. It contained weapons, cash, fake IDs, and everything else he would need to flee effectively.

Within seconds, Bucky had thrown the bag out the window, knocked down all the troops, dropped Cap's shield, and disappeared through the window himself.

"He's coming out!" Cap shouted to Falcon over the comms.

Bucky launched out onto the building's patio, four floors above street level, knocking out troops as he went. Then he leaped to the ground, landing easily, as if it were a short jump, instead of a forty-five-foot plunge.

Bucky was about to run off into the streets when suddenly—*CLANG!*—metal claws flashed out of nowhere and raked across his cybernetic metal arm. Sparks flew.

Bucky spun to see a man dressed in black armor. The armor featured a full mask with catlike ears and piercing eyes, and a necklace made of vibranium. Bucky's attacker moved fluidly and gracefully. He approached like a fierce animal— like a black panther.

Bucky and Black Panther fought viciously, throwing punch after punch and wrestling each other across the pavement.

Cap ran out onto the patio and looked down, spotting Black Panther.

"Who's the other guy?" Falcon asked Cap over the comms, still observing from far above.

"I'm about to find out," said Cap, and made the jump down to street level.

CHAPTER 7

Bucky and Black Panther continued to trade blows as Cap stuck a flawless landing near them. His plan was to split the two up, but that plan went out the window when a GSG9 chopper swooped down and opened fire. It was shooting at all three of them!

Cap dove for cover, but Bucky broke into a run to escape the attack.

Black Panther, however, neither hid nor ran. He let the armor-piercing bullets hit him. He didn't even move. He stood in a hail of bullets the way a person might stand under a shower. The attack had no effect on him.

Cap was shocked. There was only one way the man in the panther suit could withstand that onslaught. His armor had to be made of pure vibranium, the same as Cap's shield.

Black Panther glared at the helicopter's wind-shield, giving the pilot a reproving look, then he sprinted after Bucky.

Cap raced after Panther, and Falcon swooped down to follow Cap. The chase was on!

Bucky led Black Panther on a race across the city's industrial rooftops. The two figures vaulted over skylights and air ducts. Bucky was running his hard-est, but Black Panther was effortlessly keeping pace.

Not far behind were Cap and Falcon. Cap was still on foot while Falcon was flying above.

Once again, the same GSG9 helicopter flew up alongside them and started spraying them with ammo.

"Sam, can you do something about this?" asked Cap over the comms.

"Got him," said Sam confidently.

Falcon turned in midair, heading for the chopper. He tucked his wings and kicked the helicopter's tail rotor. The gunship instantly went into a spin, peeling off and flying away.

Falcon dipped down, unfurling his wings and catching the wind to glide just a few feet above the street.

Up ahead, Bucky jumped off another roof and snagged a street lamp with his metal arm. The pole bent, slowing his fall. But Black Panther dove after him, digging his claws into the side of a building to control his descent.

Then Bucky jumped onto the walkway of a busy tunnel, next to several lanes of oncoming traffic. He hurdled the barricade, racing against the cars as they whizzed by only inches away.

Black Panther and Cap followed Bucky by leaping into the traffic, too. They both began vaulting over cars, running against the current to try to catch up.

From his vantage point above the others, Falcon could see that up ahead, Bucky was entering a tunnel. "Underground causeway, southbound!" Sam shouted out to Cap, giving him Bucky's position. "I'll head around and cut him off from the other side." Sam pulled up in his wing suit and flew above the tunnel.

Black Panther disappeared into the tunnel behind Bucky, but when Cap ran for the tunnel's mouth, a GSG9 military SUV nearly clipped him. Cap jumped and turned so the shield strapped to his back would absorb the impact, cracking the SUV's windshield in a spiderweb pattern and bowing it inward.

The GSG9 soldier driving the SUV slammed on the brakes in surprise.

Cap leaped off the roof of the now stationary SUV and yanked open the driver's-side door. "Are you okay?" he asked the dazed and confused driver in German.

"Yeah, I think so," the soldier answered.

"Good," said Cap, then yanked the driver from the SUV, climbed in, and took off as fast as he could go.

Up ahead in the tunnel, Bucky was still running, weaving through traffic and trying to shake Black Panther. But Black Panther ran to the other side of the road, into traffic that was going their direction, and jumped onto one of the cars. By leaping from car to car, Black Panther steadily caught up with Bucky. He was relentless in his pursuit.

Looking back, Bucky saw that Black Panther was gaining on him. He desperately needed to do something different.

Seeing someone on a motorcycle heading toward him, Bucky stuck out his metal arm and knocked off the rider. Commandeering the bike, Bucky jumped on and gunned the engine.

Driving the SUV, Cap was able to veer around traffic. He soon caught up to Black Panther and was getting closer to Bucky's motorcycle. But as Cap passed him, Black Panther jumped on top of the SUV.

On the vehicle's roof, Black Panther waited until they were close enough to Bucky...then leaped onto the back of Bucky's motorcycle.

Bucky instantly started swinging backward, trying to knock Black Panther off the bike. Panther dodged the first couple attempts, but then Bucky slammed Panther with his metal arm. Panther fell to the pavement.

Bucky was sure Black Panther was gone for good, but he was wrong. As soon as Black Panther hit the ground, he reached out and shoved his claws into Cap's passing SUV, letting the vehicle lift him up and away.

Cap swerved but couldn't shake off Black Panther!

Bucky was nearing the tunnel's exit and looked back to see Black Panther clinging to the side of Cap's SUV. When Bucky returned his attention to the road, he was shocked to see Falcon flying into the tunnel, headed straight for him.

Bucky instantly slammed on his brakes, sending the motorcycle up on its back wheel, then swinging it around, he headed in the opposite direction.

As Bucky's motorcycle sped past him, Cap skidded to a quick stop, then put the SUV in reverse and drove backward toward the fleeing Bucky. As Falcon flew by Cap's SUV, Black Panther leaped from the vehicle onto Falcon, digging his claws into the metal wings.

"Oh, come on, man!" Falcon shouted at his surprise hitchhiker. Sam had to kick in his thrusters just to stay aloft with the added weight.

Not far ahead, Bucky was looking for another way out of the tunnel. He reached into his bag and pulled out a small metal ball. It looked insignificant, but it was actually a powerful explosive. He threw it at the ceiling of the tunnel, where it blew a massive hole in the concrete. Daylight streamed in.

Falcon instantly pulled up, using his wings to

shield himself from the explosion. That caused Black Panther to launch off of Sam, and his momentum carried him right through the fireball. The heat of the blast would have been too intense for Black Panther to bear if not for his insulating suit.

Seeing the explosion ahead, Cap leaped from the SUV, pulling out his shield and clutching it in front of him. The shield took the brunt of the impact as Cap hit the ground.

Meanwhile, Bucky swerved to avoid a car, and his bike skidded sideways. Bucky was thrown to the ground, and in under a second, Black Panther was on top of him, swinging his sharp claws.

Cap tackled Black Panther, knocking him off of Bucky. Panther's vibranium claws slashed at Cap's shield, leaving deep gashes. That was something Cap had never seen before—a weapon that could damage his supposedly indestructible shield...but then again, Panther's claws were made of the same metal.

Cap and Panther were still trading blows when, suddenly, repulsor fire pounded into the ground around them. Cap, Panther, Bucky, and Sam all looked up to see an Iron Man–inspired armor suit flying into the tunnel through the hole Bucky's explosive had created. War Machine had arrived.

"Everyone, stop!" commanded James "Rhodey" Rhodes from inside the War Machine armor.

Cap and the others looked to see that they were surrounded on all sides and above by heavily armed GSG9 troops.

"Hold your fire!" Rhodey shouted to the GSG9 soldiers as he landed.

Cap saw Bucky turn and look at the troops, seething. Bucky was clearly considering taking out as many as he could and then making a break for it. But it would never work. He would be destroyed if he tried.

Cap whispered to Bucky, "No, don't. It's what they want you to do."

Bucky didn't like it, but he understood.

"Take them all into custody," Rhodey commanded the troops. He looked Cap in the eyes and said, "I feel like I'm arresting my father." Then he turned and looked at Sam. "And my idiot brother."

As the troops went forward to make the arrests, Black Panther removed his mask, revealing his identity.

Cap and Rhodey both recognized him instantly.

It was T'Challa, prince of Wakanda.

"Someone call Ross," Rhodey said. "We've got a complication."

Wanda was intentionally not using her powers as she slammed her fists into the punching bag over and over again. She wanted to feel the impact run up her arms and into her shoulders and reverberate down her spine.

She couldn't tell if she was releasing tension or just tiring herself out.

Either way, it felt good to hit something.

But she stopped when she smelled something strange, something that reminded her of home.

Dropping her boxing gloves on the training room floor, she followed the scent into the kitchen, where Vision stood next to the stove, stirring a pot. The android—the artificial life-form that could fly and blast robots—looked remarkably out of place doing something so domestic.

"Is that paprikash?" asked Wanda, trying to peer into the cookware.

"Northern Sokovian paprikash, to be specific," said Vision, looking up at her but still stirring. "I thought it might lift your spirits."

Wanda stuck a spoon into the pot and tasted it.

It was awful.

"Yum," she said, clearly disgusted. "Spirits lifted."

Vision frowned a little. "In the interests of full disclosure," he said, "I should probably tell you that I've never actually eaten anything in my entire life."

"Scoot," Wanda said, bumping Vision with her hip and taking control of the pot.

Vision watched as she rummaged through the spices and added a few to the mix. After a moment, he said, "No one dislikes you, Wanda."

"Um...thanks?" Wanda replied.

"It's an involuntary response in their amygdala. They can't help but be afraid of you."

Wanda met Vision's eyes. "Are you afraid of me?"

"My amygdala is synthetic."

Wanda nodded. It wasn't really an answer, but she'd take it. She looked away before saying, "I used to think of myself one way, but after all this, I'm something else. *I'm still me*, I think to myself. But...that's not what everyone sees."

"Do you know that I don't know what this

is?" Vision tapped the stone set in his forehead. "I know it's not from this world, that it powered Loki's staff, gave you your abilities. But its true nature is a mystery. Yet it's still part of me. In many ways, it's my mind."

"Are you afraid of it?"

Vision considered the question. "I wish to understand it. The more I do, the less it controls me. Maybe one day, I might control it."

Wanda nodded, then took another taste from the pot. She frowned and looked at one of the spice shakers. "I don't know what this red stuff is, but it isn't paprika." She grabbed her purse from the counter. "I'm going to the store. Back in twenty minutes."

As she moved to slip past Vision, he took a small step toward her, blocking her way. "Alternatively, we could order pizza."

"Vision?" Wanda had an edge in her voice. "Are you not letting me leave?"

"It's a question of safety," the android explained.

"I can protect myself."

Vision looked down, ashamed of the words that were about to come out of his mouth. "Mr. Stark wants to avoid another public incident until the accords are on a more secure foundation."

After the incidents in Sokovia and Lagos, the Avengers wanted to keep both Wanda and Vision safe. To the public, they were more dangerous than the others. Vision knew Wanda would take that personally, even though the entire team had been involved in the devastation.

And Wanda *was* clearly hurt. "What do *you* want?"

Vision looked her in the eyes. "For people to see you as you really are."

Helicopters swept in first, ahead of the convoy. Behind them traveled a line of police and military vehicles. In the center of the line were two highly armored trucks, used to transport high-security prisoners to the international security task force headquarters in Germany.

From inside one of the trucks, Sam looked out the window at the passing city. "I've never been to Berlin before," he remarked.

"I have," Steve said grimly.

In the row of seats ahead of Cap and Sam, T'Challa sat in silence. Sam focused his attention on the African prince. "Okay, fine. I'll ask. Are you, like, superpowered, or is it just the suit?"

T'Challa remained silent.

Sam continued. "Do you fight crime? Does Wakanda even have crime?"

Cap gave Sam a look.

"What?" asked Sam. "Dude was dressed like a cat."

T'Challa finally broke his silence. "There's a world outside the Avengers," he said simply.

After a beat, Cap said, "I'm sorry about your father."

"Then why did you get in my way?"

"Because you're after the wrong man."

T'Challa shook his head. "Innocent men don't run."

Silence reigned for the rest of the trip.

When they reached the task force headquarters, Steve, Sam, and T'Challa stepped out of the truck and into the ultramodern building. They watched as a specially modified forklift pulled a cage off the other armored truck. Inside the cage was Bucky Barnes, the Winter Soldier.

"What's going to happen to him?" Steve asked as the HQ's ranking officer, Everett K. Ross, walked up to the group.

"The same thing that *should* happen to you," said Everett. "Psych evaluation and extradition."

Behind Everett was Cap's friend Sharon, who had been assigned as Everett's administrative staff. She didn't acknowledge Cap.

"What about a lawyer?" Cap asked.

Everett actually rolled his eyes at the question, then turned to issue Sharon an order. "See that their weapons are locked up." He turned back to Cap. "It's a secure facility. Only guards carry weapons."

Sam watched as Cap's shield, Black Panther's

protective suit, and his own wing suit were carried off the armored truck. "I better not look out the window and see anybody flying around in that!"

Guards led Steve, Sam, and T'Challa deeper into the building, where Black Widow was waiting. "For the record, this is what 'making things worse' looks like," she said as Cap approached.

"Bucky's still alive," Steve said. "That's not worse in my book."

Everett pulled T'Challa into a side office, away from the group. Meanwhile, Natasha followed Cap and Sam into a different room, where Tony Stark was on the phone.

"No, Romania was not accords sanctioned," Tony said into the phone. "Colonel Rhodes is supervising cleanup.... Yes, there will be consequences.... Yes, absolutely you can quote me on that—I just said it, didn't I?" Tony, clearly frustrated, hung up the phone without saying good-bye.

He turned to face Cap. "Secretary Ross wants you prosecuted. I had to give him something."

"I'm not getting my shield back, am I?" Cap asked.

"Technically, it's still government property." Tony glanced over at Sam. "The wings, too, actually."

"That's cold," Sam said.

"Warmer than jail," Natasha replied.

T'Challa used all his influence as the future king of Wakanda to pressure the collected world authorities to extradite the Winter Soldier to his country, where he would face several charges, including terrorism.

Meanwhile, Bucky was given a psychological evaluation so the authorities could try to understand his mental state. It was widely understood that the Winter Soldier program had brainwashed Bucky...but little was known about what residual effects the conditioning might have caused.

Still in the room with Tony, Cap watched a monitor showing a live feed of the evaluation. Onscreen, the doctor was asking Bucky questions, but Bucky was slow to answer and appeared confused.

"Listen," Tony said. Cap's eyes remained fixed on the monitor. "So far you haven't done anything that can't be undone."

Cap turned to look at Tony, wondering where he was going with this, and what he really wanted.

Tony shrugged. "Okay...it turns out it looks bad when Captain America doesn't sign your accords. If you come on board, we can make the last twenty-four hours legit. Barnes could be headed to a nice American psych center, instead of a Wakandan jail."

Steve worked his jaw, thinking. If it helped Bucky, maybe he would have to agree to the accords. Tony saw Cap's resolve waver and kept pressing his advantage. "I need you, Steve," Tony said imploringly.

"I'm not saying it's impossible," said Steve, "but there'd need to be safeguards."

Tony brightened. Now they were getting somewhere. "Tell me what gets it done. Documents can be amended. Once we put out the public relations fire, I'll find a way to have you and Wanda reinstated."

Steve tensed. "What's this about Wanda?"

Tony hesitated momentarily and then tried to act casual. "Nothing. She's great."

Cap fixed him with a look.

"She's currently confined to the compound," Tony admitted.

Cap's look turned to disappointment.

Tony rolled his eyes. "It's a hundred acres with a screening room and a lap pool. There are worse ways to protect her."

"Is that what you're telling yourself? That it's protection?" Cap shook his head. "It's imprisonment."

"It's the best option available," said Tony with exasperation. "She's not an American citizen, and they don't give visas to weapons of mass destruction."

"She's just a kid," said Cap accusingly.

"People just want to feel safe," Tony said lamely.

Steve stared at Tony for a long time.

Finally, he said, "Well, you're doing a great job so far."

EPILOGUE

By taking Cap, Falcon, and the Winter Soldier into custody, Tony believed he'd be ending the Avenger-on-Avenger conflict.

But he was wrong.

Captain America was sure that Bucky had been set up, forced to take the fall for acts of terrorism of which he was innocent. What Cap wasn't sure about was why it had been done and who had done it . . . but he knew he had to find out.

The problem was twofold.

First, Cap didn't know whom to trust. Whoever was framing Bucky could easily be someone on the inside. Cap hadn't forgotten that S.H.I.E.L.D. itself, the organization that had first conceived of the Avengers Initiative, had been exposed as a front for Hydra. After going through something like that, it was hard for Cap to trust anyone.

Second, even those whom Cap knew he could trust might not believe him. Iron Man was a case in point. Cap and Tony had fought side by side against some of the worst threats Earth had ever faced. Cap knew he could trust Tony . . . but that didn't mean that he and Tony would always agree. In fact, they often didn't.

Tony didn't know Bucky. He didn't have the firm belief in him that Cap did.

So those loyal to Cap would stay on his side. And those loyal to Iron Man would stay on Tony's side.

For the time being, at least, the Avengers were going to be fighting against one another.

Their civil war was far from over.

TURN THE PAGE FOR AN EXCITING PREVIEW OF

MARVEL CINEMATIC UNIVERSE
PHASE TWO

CHAPTER 1

It was a fine cool morning to be jogging on the National Mall in Washington, DC. Sam Wilson planned to put in his miles and then he had to get to work at the VA rehab facility. He liked running on mornings like these, before the heat settled in and DC turned into a steam bath. He wasn't thinking about much, just enjoying the groove of the run, the feeling of his body getting loose. He heard a voice from behind him. "On your left."

Sam nodded. It was standard runner's courtesy to let someone know when you were going to pass them on a path. But the other guy was moving fast. Really fast. Almost at a sprint. He shot ahead of Sam and made a turn, disappearing behind the Lincoln Memorial. If he kept up that pace, he wasn't going to get very far. Sam decided he must be doing some kind of interval workout. Sprints, then walks. Something like that.

Sam's standard loop around the National Mall was almost exactly four miles. The first time he saw the fast guy was about a mile and a half into it. Then, before he reached the three-mile mark, he heard it again. "On your left."

There he went again. "Uh-huh. On my left. Got it," Sam said. He considered himself to be in pretty good shape, but this guy was Olympic level. Unless he was catching a ride or something. He watched the other runner go, and picked up his own pace. A little competition was good. He could go faster and he didn't like having other runners show him up. His lungs started to burn and he could feel the muscles in his legs burn, too. This wasn't just a regular jog anymore.

When he was a few hundred yards short of the complete loop, he heard footsteps again. "Don't say it. Don't you say it," he said, trying to go faster, but he was pretty worn out.

"On your left." The other runner went by at the same robotic near-sprint.

"Come on!" Sam said. He started to sprint, too. When he got to the four-mile mark, he staggered off the path and sat down by a tree, panting. It had been a long time since he'd run that hard.

The other guy had stopped, too. He strolled back over to Sam, barely out of breath. Now that

Sam saw his face, he started to figure out how the guy had kept up that crazy pace. "Need a medic?" he asked Sam.

"I need a new set of lungs," Sam said, half-serious. "Dude, you just ran, like, thirteen miles in thirty minutes."

"I guess I got a late start."

"Really? You should be ashamed of yourself. You should take another lap. Did you just take it? I assume you just took it." Sam laughed at himself.

"What unit you with?" Mister Fast asked.

"Fifty-Eighth Pararescue. But now I'm working down at the VA." Sam got to his feet and extended a hand. "Sam Wilson."

"Steve Rogers."

"I kind of put that together." Sam couldn't believe he was talking to Captain America. "Must have freaked you out, coming home after the whole defrosting thing."

"It takes some getting used to. It's good to meet you, Sam." Captain America turned to go.

Sam was a little bit starstruck and a little bit curious. He also felt like maybe he'd put his foot in his mouth by bringing up the defrosting thing. "It's your bed, right?" he called out.

Steve turned back. "What's that?"

"Your bed, it's too soft. When I was over there, I'd sleep on the ground, use rocks for pillows like a caveman. Now I'm home, lying in my bed, and it's like…"

"Lying on a marshmallow," Steve finished.

"Feel like I'm gonna sink right to the floor," Sam said.

Steve nodded. "How long?"

"Two tours. You must miss the good old days, huh?"

Steve thought about it. "Well, things aren't so bad. Food's a lot better. We used to boil everything. No polio is good. Internet, so helpful. I've been reading that a lot, trying to catch up."

I bet you spend a lot of time trying to catch up, Sam thought. He had an idea. "Marvin Gaye, 1972, *Trouble Man* soundtrack," he said. "Everything you missed jammed into one album."

"I'll put it on the list." Sam saw him write it down in a little spiral notebook. Then Steve's phone chirped. He looked at his screen and said, "All right, Sam, duty calls."

"Thanks for the run."

"If that's what you want to call running," Steve joked.

Sam laughed. "Oh, that's how it is?"

"Oh, that's how it is."

"Okay." Sam waved. "Any time you want to stop by the VA, make me look awesome in front of the girl at the front desk, just let me know."

"I'll keep it in mind," Steve said with a grin.

With a rev of its overpowered engine, a black sports car pulled up to the curb nearby. The driver was a young redheaded woman Sam recognized immediately: Agent Natasha Romanoff of S.H.I.E.L.D. *Holy smokes*, he thought. *This sure is better than bumping into senators while you're trying to cross Pennsylvania Avenue.* "Hey, fellas," Romanoff said. "Either one of you know where the Smithsonian is? I'm here to pick up a fossil."

Steve glanced over at Sam as he walked to the car. He figured Sam would be checking Natasha out and he was right. She was hard to ignore. "That's hilarious."

As he got in the car, he saw that Natasha was also checking Sam out. "How you doing?" Sam said.

She gave him a little smile. "Hey."

Steve grinned at him. "Can't run everywhere," he said.

As the car squealed away into traffic, Sam Wilson said to himself, "No, you can't."

Man, he thought. *I just met two of the Avengers.*

But he still had to go home, get a shower, and get to work. Life went on.

CHAPTER 2

S.T.R.I.K.E. team leader Brock Rumlow briefed Cap and Natasha as they flew in a Quinjet over the Indian Ocean. "Target is a mobile satellite launch platform, the *Lemurian Star*. They were sending up their last payload when pirates took them, ninety-three minutes ago." Rumlow was working on a touch screen in the Quinjet's passenger compartment. He showed the ship and then its location on the map, close to the Indian coast.

"Any demands?" Steve asked.

"Billion and a half."

"Why so steep?"

"Because it's S.H.I.E.L.D.'s," Rumlow said.

That changed things. This wasn't an ordinary hijacking. "So it's not off course," Steve said. "It's trespassing."

"I'm sure they have a good reason," Natasha said.

"You know, I'm getting a little tired of being Fury's janitor."

"Relax. It's not that complicated."

"How many pirates?" Steve asked Rumlow.

"Twenty-five. Top mercs led by this guy." Rumlow pulled up a dossier on the screen. "Georges Batroc. Ex-DGSE, Action Division. He's at the top of Interpol's Red Notice. Before the French demobilized him, he had thirty-six kill missions. This guy's got a rep for maximum casualties."

"Hostages?"

"Oh, mostly techs. One officer. Jasper Sitwell." A photo of Sitwell appeared on the screen. "They're in the galley."

Steve knew Jasper Sitwell. He wasn't usually in the field. "What's Sitwell doing on a launch ship?" he wondered aloud.

Steve considered the layout of the ship and the location of the galley where the hostages were. Everything seemed pretty straightforward. "All right, I'm gonna sweep the deck and find Batroc. Nat, you kill the engines and wait for instructions." He looked at Rumlow. "Rumlow, you sweep aft, find the hostages, get them to the life-pods, get them out. Let's move."

"S.T.R.I.K.E., you heard the cap," Rumlow said. "Gear up."

"Secure channel seven," Steve said into his wrist mic, testing the frequency he would use on the operation.

"Seven secure," Natasha echoed. "Did you do anything fun Saturday night?"

"Well, all the guys from my barbershop quartet are dead, so, no, not really."

"Coming up on the drop zone, Cap," Rumlow said from up front.

"You know, if you ask Kristen from Statistics out, she'd probably say yes," Natasha said. Lately she'd started a campaign to get him to date more. Or at all.

Steve knew she was right about Kristen from Statistics. "That's why I don't ask," he said. The Quinjet's rear ramp opened up, exposing a stormy night sky.

"Too shy, or too scared?"

"Too busy!" Cap jumped out the back of the plane.

Rumlow and his second-in-command, Jack Rollins, saw Cap jump. "Was he wearing a parachute?" Rollins asked.

"No," Rumlow said with an admiring smile. "No, he wasn't."

CHAPTER 3

Steve fell through the stormy night toward the hijacked ship, then veered away and somersaulted at the last moment so he hit the water feet-first. The icy shock up his legs felt good, like the first little jab to the face when you were sparring. It woke you up, let you know it was time to focus on the mission. He'd fallen from a few hundred feet, and went pretty deep. He surfaced, climbed the side of the ship's hull, vaulted the railing, and then landed softly behind an unsuspecting mercenary on patrol.

Steve grabbed him from behind and covered his mouth, putting him in a chokehold until he was unconscious. Then he lowered the mercenary to the deck. He needed to keep up the element of surprise as long as he could.

He went counterclockwise around the deck of the ship, taking out the mercenaries as he found them. He used exactly as much force as was necessary to stop them from sounding the alarm.

Everything went fine right up until he had made an almost complete circuit of the ship. Then, just as he began to turn into the middle of the deck to get inside and head for the galley, he skidded to a halt. One of the mercenaries had him covered with an automatic rifle. "Don't move!" he shouted.

Steve froze. Out of the corner of his eye, he saw another armed mercenary. They had overlapping fields of fire and he had no place to run. He could probably take them down, but he was going to lose some blood doing it.

Then there was a soft pop and the nearest mercenary collapsed. Before he even hit the deck, the second man also fell. A moment later Brock Rumlow dropped out of the sky, parachute trailing behind him over the deck. He held the rifle he'd used to drop the two mercenaries. *Good shooting*, Steve thought. It wasn't easy to be accurate when you were hanging from a parachute on a windy night and shooting at a moving target on the deck of a ship, which was also moving. Rumlow was among S.H.I.E.L.D.'s best.

"Thanks," Cap said.

"Yeah," Rumlow said with a grin. "You seemed pretty helpless without me."

Natasha and the rest of the team dropped around them and together they all started off to the next mission objective: find Sitwell and also find Georges Batroc. "What about the nurse who lives across the hall from you?" Natasha asked Steve as they walked. "She seems kind of nice."

Her name was Kate, and Natasha was right. She was nice. Steve appreciated what Natasha was trying to do, but his mind wasn't on romance right then. "Secure the engine room, then find me a date."

"I'm multitasking," she said, and vaulted a railing before dropping down to the lower deck, where the engine room was.

CHAPTER 4

In the galley, the mercenaries were getting impatient. "I told Batroc," one of them said in French, "if we want to make S.H.I.E.L.D. pay us, start sending them bodies now!" He walked up and down the row of hostages. They were all sitting on the floor, hands and feet tied. "I have a bullet for someone.... You want a bullet in your head?" He kicked Jasper Sitwell's foot. "Move that foot—you want a bullet in the head?"

Sitwell just looked at him. He knew S.H.I.E.L.D. would have launched a rescue mission. It was only a matter of time.

Steve got to the lower level of the ship's bridge tower and shot a small, sticky disk up to the bridge window. The disk contained a microphone that let him in on what the mercenaries were saying. "I don't like waiting," one of them was complaining in French.

"Call Durand," another said. "I want this ship ready to move when the ransom comes."

There was a pause, and Steve heard the first mercenary say, "Start the engines." Then he hung up the phone.

Down in the engine room, the mercenary who had taken the call turned to get the engines started. He froze when he saw Natasha Romanoff, smiling at him. "Hey, sailor," she said.

In the galley, the restless mercenary got sick of shouting at the hostages. "All right, I've waited long enough," he announced, and pounded on the door. "Hey! Find Batroc. If I don't hear anything in two minutes, I start killing them!"

"I'll find him," the mercenary outside called back.

But when he turned around, he walked right into Brock Rumlow's Taser. He went down without a sound. The rest of the S.T.R.I.K.E. team waited with Rumlow for the order to go in.

Outside, Cap was watching the bridge and still

listening in. He knew Batroc was up there when one of the mercenaries said, "Radio silence from S.H.I.E.L.D., Batroc."

"S.T.R.I.K.E. in position," Rumlow reported.

It was time to go in. "Natasha, what's your status?" She didn't answer. "Status, Natasha."

"Hang on!" Natasha snapped. She was a little busy with the last three mercenaries in the engine room area. She took them out with a combination of unarmed strikes and electrical jolts from the stingers built into the wrists of her uniform. Then she got back to Steve. "Engine room secure."

Inside the galley, the mercenaries got ready as the two minutes ran out. "Time is up," the leader said. "Who dies first?" He pointed at a random agent. "You!"

Then there was a series of sharp cracks as the galley's windows shattered by S.T.R.I.K.E. snipers hanging outside. The mercenaries all dropped. A split second later, the galley door blew off its hinges, and with a single shot, Brock Rumlow took out the leader who had started the two-minute countdown.

He fell right in front of Jasper Sitwell, who looked at him and said, "I told you. S.H.I.E.L.D. doesn't negotiate."